The Captain's Hat

Anita Williams

Illustrated by
Timothy Banks

JOURNEY BOOKS™
Greenville, South Carolina

Library of Congress Cataloging-in-Publication data

Williams, Anita, 1926-
    The Captain's hat / Anita Williams ; illustrated by Tim Banks.
       p. cm.
    Summary: After he and his American friend Spud explore along the
Big River, romp through the Brazilian jungle, and meet an old sailor
who lives in a ship scuttled on a beach, Pedro finally earns the honor
of wearing a Captain's hat.
    ISBN 1-57954-330-4
    [1. Ships—Fiction. 2. Rivers—Fiction. 3. Jungles—Fiction.
4. Brazil—Fiction.] I. Banks, Timothy, ill. II. Title.

PZ7.W65582 Cap 2000
[Fic]—dc21   99-052817

The Captain's Hat
Editor: Gloria Repp
Project Editor: Debbie L. Parker
Designed by Duane A. Nichols and Noelle Snyder

© 2000 Journey Books
Published by Bob Jones University Press
Greenville, SC 29614

ISBN 1-57954-330-4

15 14 13 12 11 10 9 8 7 6 5 4 3 2 1

To children—everywhere—
who wish to wear a Captain's hat
—A.W.

To my grandparents
—T.B.

Contents

Chapter 1

Pedro

Pedro's kitchen at seven o'clock . . .
Coffee and hot milk steamed.
Hard-crusted bread waited on a blue plate.

He curled himself up onto a tall stool.
Pretty pink Leja, cheeks bright as cherries,
smiled at him.

"Good morning, Pedro."

She tilted the milk pitcher.
Hot bubbles oozed into his cup.
White milk, dark coffee—a swirly look.

"You slept like a sailor, did you?"
she said.

"Mmmm-hmmmm." Sailors' ships
and rolling rivers romped the night
in Pedro's dreams.

His knife slid butter across bread crust.
Dollops of jelly plopped onto that.

"A fine day for play," said Leja.

Pedro grinned. He liked their mornings
together in the pleasant kitchen.
While Poppa and Momma traveled,
Leja minded him well.

They spoke of the Big River.

"Such washy waves, such bossy boats,"
she murmured.

"Spud's here for the whole summer,"
he said. "Likes our river, likes our forest."

Clapping sounded outside.
In Brazil, instead of knocking on the door,
people clap at the gate.

Leja laughed. "Must be Spud, that stringy-
haired boy. Hair as yellow as the corn
in our garden."

Pedro's milky breakfast drink had vanished.
Not a dot of jelly remained on his plate.
He made for the door.

Leja said, "Stay clear of lively horses.
Watch when you cross streets.
Don't get mud on your clothes.
You two, be careful around that river
. . . you hear?"

"Yes, Leja!"

All the children had respect for the Big River,
even its gullies and little streams.
It had splashy boats. The smoking peanut cart.

Dockworkers bumping about.
Roly-poly barrels that made such noise.

The two boys swung up on the gate.
There, breezes smelled sweeter.
The sky looked like a sea, it was so blue.

Wagon wheels creaked.
Gangling Mr. Bottle Man sat like a post on his
high seat. Sitting tall, he'd catch any glint or
sparkle. His glance caught up Pedro and Spud.
The wagon slowed.

> "It's Wednesday," he said.
> "The road's strewn with useful items!
> Bottles, rags, burnt sticks, cracked cups."
> His happy laugh rang out.
> "Come along, friends."

Their wagon clip-clopped down the street.

> "We'll take your rags and tags,"
> called out Mr. Bottle Man.
> "Your hopeless pieces. Your tatters,
> tidbits, your bent, your scrappy . . ."

People smiled and handed up their gifts.
A pillow with loose stuffing,
a rag doll with no hair,

a greasy auto clutch.
He beamed upon the collection.

At a sticky spot, the mule balked.
Newspapers, bottles, pipes, buttons,
flopped into a pile in the wagon.

Pedro slid deep into the scuttle.
Spud clung to the edges.
Mr. Bottle Man laughed merrily.

"Such a mess," he said.

The two squiggled up and out.

"Thanks, Mr. Bottle Man.
We'll get off at the waterfront, please."

He chuckled.

"I know why you want off there.
You want to see big and little ships
come chugging in; see them heaving
on the muddy, blackish water."

"It's so! Thank you!"
They were off and running.

Chapter 2

The Tub

A big black ship was bumping about in the water.

"Owwww!" cried Spud.
"That's as fine a vessel as ever I've seen."

"Where's the Captain?"
Pedro stretched to see.
"What's he look like?"

Pedro could imagine.
"He's strong and brave and brown—
and wide-eyed from staring down
a mean fish."

"You think this ship's had pirates?"

"No," said Pedro.
"The Captain made them leave."

The water puzzled Spud.
"This river looks like cola. Like tea."

Two big waves blew up like a windstorm.
The boys squealed and tumbled back.

A fishing boat was rocking in.
The red, muscled fisherman with yellow teeth
set eyes on them.

    "Hey, landlubbers," he hollered.
    "Come, help haul in fish."

River wind blew suddenly cool.
Their bare feet splashed over the washed pier.
Silt, weeds, and flower rags floated in river foam.
River birds dived.

    "Careful stepping that plank!"
    called the man.

It looked wet and shivery.
They scampered onto it and over.

Their cold feet swamped down
onto the boat's soppy bottom,
onto mud and grass.

Hooks, lines, spinners, and bait lay about.
Scents came—fishy water and soap,
and crawly little fish.

"The white tub, mates."
The fisherman pointed.
"Haul the tub to market."

"Owww," squealed Spud.
"Must be ten million fish!"

The tub was heavy.
The two boys and all the fish
got a sunburn on the way.
They settled the tub onto a concrete slab,
among fish tables.

The fisherman with yellow teeth said,
"Fine work, mates."
He handed them money
and pointed to a smoking cart.
"Hot meat pies. Makes a fine lunch, no?"

The pie man's twitchy mustache wriggled.
"Peppery hot pastries?"
Carefully, he handed over the wraps
and accepted their money.

"Dee-licious," said Pedro.

Meat, green herbs and pepper . . .
the pastries were pie-flaky good.
Pedro and Spud licked the greasy paper
and dropped tatters into a bucket.

"What's that big ship carrying?"
Spud gazed at it seriously.

"Farm machines," said Pedro.

"Molasses," said Spud.

"Tea," said Pedro.

"Saddles, swords, spears," said Spud.
"Engines, car parts."

Sailors scurried around on deck.
In the midst of those blue britches—
an important person, distinctive,
a person of great dignity.

"Who's that?" said Spud.

Pedro saw. "The Captain!
He's wearing the Captain's hat."

The elegant, handsome piece tipped exactly right.
It tipped as would the hat of a Captain.

With authority and honor, it rested on the
Captain's dark hair.

"What a hat!"

Pedro couldn't take his eyes off it.
The sun sparkled everything gold.

"Spud?"

"Mmmm-hmmmm."

"Someday, I—Pedro—
will wear a Captain's hat."

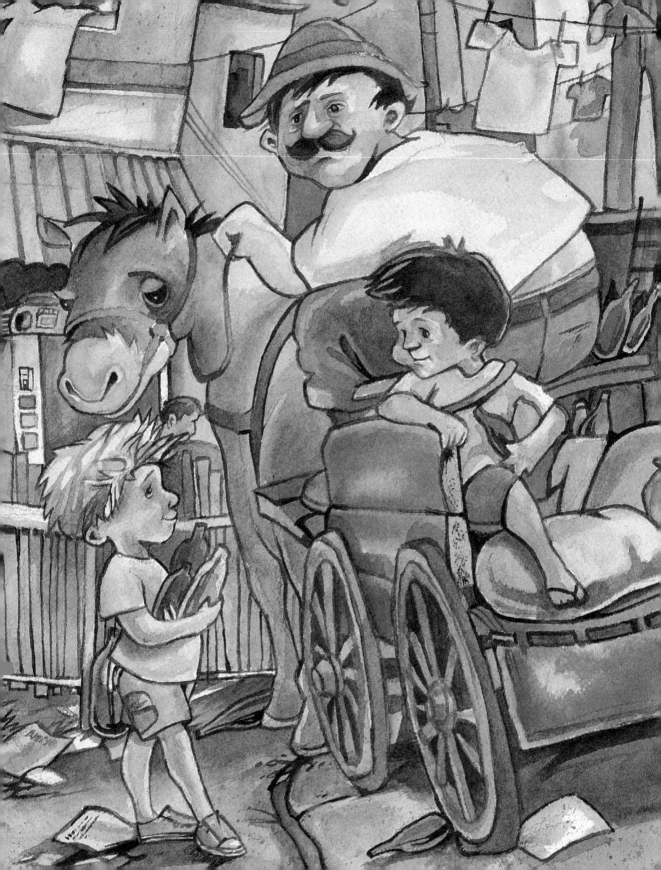

Chapter 3

Forest Trails

Pedro and Spud climbed the gate early and sat.
Wagon wheels creaked.

"Mr. Bottle Man's rolling in," said Pedro.

Seeing them, Mr. Bottle Man chuckled.
"Road's strewn with useful pieces.
Bent cans, scratched bottles, cracked cups . . ."

His happy laugh rang out.
"Anything mendable . . . bendable.
Fill my wagon with useful pieces."

The wagon rattled past nice shops.

"Delicious," said Spud. "I smell
cola, frozen pops, and Irish tea."

They sniffed so hard that they fell into the rubble.
It was dusty and rather scratchy.

THE CAPTAIN'S HAT

The wagon clattered past the waterfront
to a path of silky flowers.

"We'll get off here, please."

As they swung down, Mr. Bottle Man said,
"Mind the river. Don't fall in.
Watch out for bitey insects."

The wagon wobbled away.

Spud turned round and round.
"Where's the river?" he asked.

"Can't see it," said Pedro.
"Trees and tangle are in the way."

But the river wasn't far. They heard clanks,
shouts, and splashes. Beyond, there showed
a trail of ferns and blooms. They tacked onto it.

Soon, the doubtful trail mushed to mud.
Wet weeds showered them. Trees dripped.

"Pedro, why is it always so
soppy wet here?"

"Just is."

"Let's find a dry spot."

"Not any."

They chanced upon a knotty log
 and sat upon it by a pool.

They rubbed off mud and listened to birds jabber.
The water's lovely circles rounded out and out
into more lovely circles. Fish played water games.

The trail led off to a rich, deeper forest—a mystery!
They stumped along it and chased a butterfly
and met a parrot. In the tangle of green thickness,
they stood tiny.

"Pedro, we lost?"

"N-no." But the river was gone,
as far as Pedro could tell.

"Every green thing kinks, knots, or curls,"
said Spud. "You see how the little stuff twines
around the big stuff?"

Pedro laughed.
"Grubs smash under my feet."

The forest trail narrowed.
Spud rubbed his face.

THE CAPTAIN'S HAT

"It's hot, humid, and I'm dripping wet,"
he said. "Never have I been more
positive of anything. Pedro—we're lost."

Pedro looked about.
"I th-think we're downriver."

They gazed in dismay at the trees.

Spud groaned. "We're captured—
prisoners. We're trapped."

"Sometimes . . ."
Pedro spoke dreamily.
"Ships get lost at sea."

"So? What do they
do then?"

"The captains read charts. They hurry,
and twirl the big wheel."

At a bog, Spud looked about.
"Well, I've twirled round and round.
I don't know where I began or where I ended."

"That's okay, Spud."

They listened to the hot sighs of the jungle.
After buzzes, a whoosh, and crackling,
the forest hushed.

Chapter 4

An Uncommon Beach

"Listen, Spud. Hear that? The river! Hear?"

They cleared small trees and short logs
and scrubbed through brush,
as if flying through feathers.

Just beyond a thickness, the river sparkled.

"Oh!"

The merry river rolled.

"We weren't really lost," said Spud.
"Just crossways . . . turned about."

The river romped, and Pedro welcomed it.
He looked north, south, east, west.
Still, he didn't know where they were.

To the right lay a path, slightly worn.
They scampered onto it. The weeds were shorter
and less stubby. Sand spread about.

> Then Spud gulped and said,
> "What an uncommon beach!
> Bare and white as any bone!"

> He looked up, down. "Clear as a whistle.
> No bottles or cans; no frozen pop sticks."
> He kicked the sand into a flurry.
> "The sand's different too."

> "It's not a people beach," said Pedro.

> "It's deserted, Pedro. Cleared out.
> Forsaken."

Sand sifted over their toes.

> "Look, Spud—up ahead—
> the river bends. Let's go!"

Almost at once, a splatter of banana trees
and palms sparkled.

> "What's there?" cried Spud, shrinking back.
> "Am I seeing a dream? Is that real?"

Pedro gulped. What he saw was as real as any
ship that ever had sailed the seven seas.

The Big River had tossed up a ship—
a huge dark ship onto the beach.

"A-abandoned," stammered Spud.

"Rusted and streaked."

"Pirates attacked it?"

"No. I th-think it's a steamer."

"See that anchor?" asked Spud.

"Yes, and look . . ."

Sturdy ladder steps climbed to the deck—
these surprised them most.

Spud whispered, "Whoever has seen a
parked ship, with steps going up it?"

"Unheard of," Pedro said.

The dark ship seemed to shudder.
Its presence smelled of dark rust and river wash.
Beached there, it was a terrible mystery.

"You suppose it's got a Captain?"
Pedro said.

The Big River had tossed up a ship . . .

Spud kept eyeing those steps.
"I can't resist any climbing ladder, Pedro.
Hurry!"

They darted to it. Once there, it seemed high—
and scary.

"Hullo!"
From the height, a voice startled them.
"Hullo there!"

Leaning over the top rail stood a skinny Grandpoppa.
Sparkly eyeglasses skimmed his nose.
Breezes puffed out a blowzy shirt.
A twitch of gray hair circled his head,
and a bit grew on his face.

"We—" Pedro's voice sounded tiny,
like a speck. His right foot held firm
on the first ladder step.

Now came a round Grandmomma to stand beside
the Grandpoppa. Her apron flounced.
Her gray hair pulled up above a rosy face.
Seeing their surprise, she laughed.

The Grandpoppa bent, and his eyeglasses
looked like goggles.

"This is our home," he called merrily.
"Come on up, and welcome."

"Scrub sand off your shoes,"
said the Grandmomma.

Almost at once they tumbled onto the gray deck,
dazzled and wondering.

"Names, please," said the Grandmomma.

"Pedro."

"Spud."

The Grandpoppa's eyeglasses toppled.
The Grandmomma's rosy face shone.

"I hope you like our ship house,"
they said, speaking almost together.

"Yes, ma'am. Yes, sir."

Pedro looked across the long, wide, gray deck.
He saw ledges, rounds, squares, even triangles.
A solitary lifeboat hung there.
Ruffles of curtains fluttered at the cabin windows.

"Lovely," said Spud. "But why
is your home so high?"

"One must climb high to find a good
view," said the Grandpoppa.
He circled his arm about his rosy wife.
He poked his shirt and said, "I'm Mr. Sails."

"And," said the smiling Grandmomma,
"I'm Mrs. Sails."

Chapter 5

The Galley

The twinkly Grandpoppa beamed.
Sunshine glimmered on his eyeglasses.

"Welcome, mates!"
He reached out and shook their hands.

Really, thought Pedro, the man resembled no
Captain at all. The smiling Grandmomma
wore a twist in her gray hair.

"You didn't think to see a ship house on
a sandy beach?"

"No, ma'am," Pedro replied politely.

He looked about the wide, blue-gray deck.
That faded lifeboat . . . who had tossed the little
craft into the waves? Who had sailed in it?
He admired the iron rings holding it.

"Now, Mrs. Sails,"—the Grandpoppa winked—"I'm thinking these mates are hungry. Did I see chocolaty cookies in the galley?"

"You did!" And she was gone.

He chuckled, nodding toward a tall rocker.
It had curving rims and a high, straight back.

"A rocking chair on a ship
—you think that unusual?"

Spud sat and rocked,
sparkling orange and gold.
He sputtered in joy, then
he gave Pedro a turn.

Pedro felt small in the high rocker.
He rocked, rocked high, higher,
glimpsing sky, catching treetops.

He cruised the river.
Such fun was that, he journeyed out to sea.

He climbed rigging, and up there, gulped in air.
River air tasted of forest, the sea of briny salt.
Deep, deep-down, the water roared.

The rocker slowed. Standing, he felt airy and
light. A glow warmed him.

Spud gazed east and stared west.
He glared north and frowned south.

"Where are neighbors?" he said.

"Neighbors!" Mr. Sails chuckled.
"Monkeys, parrots, turtles, frogs—
those are our neighbors.
Birds sing. Parrots discuss the
encyclopedia. Monkeys argue about
everything."

Mr. Sails stopped and closed his eyes,
breathing deeply.
"Off to the galley, mates—
the kitchen!" he explained.

Warm, sweet scents stirred
in the smallish room.
In the center stood a wooden block of table
with low ledges winding about it.

"So your cup and plate won't slide,"
said Mrs. Sails.

They sat in stuck-down seats
at the stuck-down table.

A cookie platter was heaped with squares, rounds,
and ship-windows. Milk foamed in two glasses.
Tea steamed from two cups.
They munched and sipped.

Pedro ate two rounds and two ship-windows.
"Where's the wheel?" he said.

"Can we get to the bottom deck?"
wondered Spud.

"Did ever a wave come this high?"
asked Pedro.

"Give me five minutes in that engine
room," begged Spud.

"Listen to them!" said Mrs. Sails.
"These chocolate cookies have
too much chocolate!"

She nodded to the boys. "You'll see.
Mr. Sails keeps our ship—
as you might say—afloat.
He owns clever tools: hammers, drills,
bits and pieces, and some dandy handsaws."

Mr. Sails laughed.
"She's always saying,
'Mr. Sails, get the broom.' "

Pedro gazed around the galley.
He saw pots, pans, knives,
and forks hung on pegs.
A water jug sparkled.
There sat a small stove.

"Why do you live on a ship?"
asked Spud.

Tea mist steamed Mr. Sails's eyeglasses.
"Where else could you find such a marvelous,
natural place to live?"

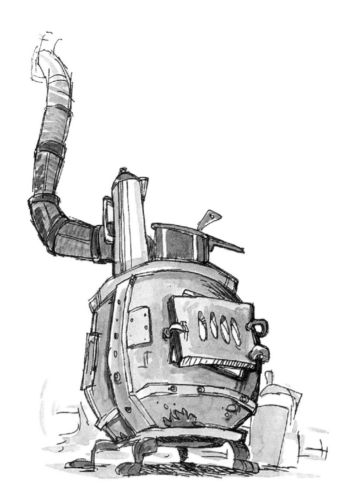

Pedro drank his milk and wondered.

Ships sail on rivers and seas.

Sailboats rock, and canoes glide.

But—this ship neither sailed nor cruised.

> Gazing at the Grandpoppa, he asked,
> "Where's your hat?"

"His hat?" Mrs. Sails giggled.
"He's got a washtub of hats.
A holey blue one, a streaked yellow,
a wrinkled red."

"Don't forget the muddy brown one,
and the green," said Mr. Sails.

"I like your sea name," said Pedro.

"You truly, honestly sailed?" said Spud.

"Yes, mate . . . with Mrs. Sails beside me.
We sailed lakes, rivers, seas.
When wind ripped sails, she mended."

"Did this ship have sailors?" asked Pedro.

"Sure, mate." Mr. Sails smiled.
"A sailor turning the ship wheel.
Two in the engine room."

"In the galley—the cook," said Mrs. Sails.
She smoothed her hair.
"The Captain—now that man had to
know all . . . and had to do all."

"Did he wear a hat?" Pedro asked.

"Certainly!" Mrs. Sails laughed.
"He wouldn't want to get sunburned,
would he?"

Chapter 6

Storm

That night a windy storm
blew around Pedro's house.
Rain pounded, raindrops slathered.
Thunder rumbled, lightning streaked.

But the bluster scared Pedro only a little.
Mostly he thought about ships at sea.

Often Poppa said, "Pray for all the sailors at sea."
After this night, Pedro thought, Mrs. Sails
might have extra work to do.
Thinking so, Pedro slept till morning.

He told Leja of the ship house,
the grinny Grandpoppa and rosy Grandmomma—
and she stood amazed.

"Oh yes," she recalled. "They sailed
the river and sailed the sea."

Syrupy dark coffee drizzled into Pedro's cup,
then hot bubbly milk.

"People visit them frequently.
They do small boat repairs.
Love having company," Leja said.

"She gave us round and ship-window cookies,"
said Pedro. "Milk too."

Leja smiled. "What a welcome!"

Outside, car wheels sloshed over bricks.

Leja looked up.
"Of course," she murmured,
"it's the bread wagon."

Pedro's milky drink disappeared.
He hurried to the gate. Through the mist
he could barely see the bread wagon.

It turned about and two shiny headlights poked
beams toward him. Wheels chunked off mud.
The wagon brought its sweet, warm scent
to Pedro's gate.

"Good morning, friend!"
High and bold sat Spud.

"An early bird catches the worm, friend."
Mr. Bread Man slowed the wagon.
"Hop in."

Pedro scooted in next to Spud.
Scents came, of sugar cane and orange butter.
Their driver whistled.

Rain seemed fitting for horn-beeping
and gear-grinding. Wheels smashed
palm tree rags. Broken limbs got a bumper shove.
Telephone poles dripped.
Drenched autos wobbled past.

"Even the birds are all wet and ruffled."
Spud laughed. "Why's it always so
soppy wet here?"

"Just is."

Houses were well washed. A newspaper boy
struggled to keep his papers dry.
A yellow dog barked. At many a gate,
Mr. Bread Man left fine loaves of bread.

They sloshed past a low hill.
Tall sugar cane dripped. Fields flooded.
It looked to Pedro that a large pitcher cloud
had upturned.

"I'm caved . . . hollow . . . totally
starving," Spud said.

"Oh, oh! We can't have that!"
boomed Mr. Bread Man.

He brought forth two new loaves, warm on waxy
paper. Jam and butter scented their crusts.

"Here, friends. I call these my middle-
sized loaves," he said with pride.
"Taste, test, give me your opinion."

"Middle-size?" repeated Spud.

"Yes, smaller than big,
but bigger than small."

Spud said, "Golden, crusty,
toothsome, delightful."

Tasty, tempting, and almost round,
Pedro thought.

The wagon rumbled onto a rutted road.
Weeds shook off raindrops.
Wet trees tangled into a huge wet net.

"I knew it!" burst out Spud. "Same weeds,
same road ruts—and a coconut tree.
This is the way to the ship house."

"What ship house? Oh—the ship scuttled on
a sandy beach? Of course . . ."
Mr. Bread Man grew thoughtful.

Soppy rags of weeds poked at their wheels.
Air turned bittersweet.

> "Are you acquainted?" asked Spud.

> "Do I know Mr. and Mrs. Sails?
> Certainly! Fine folk.
> Ahhh. I dislike climbing steps.
> If you two will deliver . . ."

His long arm reached around a round brown loaf.

The shoreline curved, and the ship's dark shadows
fell across them. Their wheels swished onto grit.
They slid on leaves, and stopped.

Pedro and Spud got out.

> "Good wishes," said Mr. Bread Man,
> and he drove off.

The storm had washed the ship.
Palm rags were flung,
bananas scattered.

What a soaking, Pedro thought, charmed.
Raindrops danced on that single lifeboat.
Ropes lay sodden. Rails glistened.

> "Where's Mr. Sails?" he said.

"He's usually sweeping the deck,"
murmured Spud.

The ship house was dark and silent.
Pedro and Spud stood on the warm sand,
gazing up.

"It's too quiet."
Pedro feared something was wrong.

Chapter 7

Red Rub

"Oh, mates, step lively!"
The Grandmomma leaned over the rail,
looking needful. "Step lively now!"

Pedro skittered up, Spud just behind.
Pedro handed over the bread.

"Thank you," she said. "But, mates,
you must make a little journey for us!"
"Yes, ma'am. Anything you wish,"
said Pedro.

It surprised him to see Mr. Sails hunkered down
in Mrs. Sails' rocking chair, looking red, rumpled,
and his shirt falling half off his shoulder.

"Had a breezy blow at dawn,"
he muttered. "I climbed the ropes."

"That prankish wind blew him down."
Mrs. Sails sighed. "Whipped him
round like a burlap bag."

"It's my shoulder," he groaned.
"I need Red Rub."

"Medicine," Mrs. Sails said.
"Comes in a red bottle.
Rubs away the pain."

Splashes sounded, and Mrs. Sails cried,
"Banana raft!"

A wooden raft rushed by, spread with great stalks
of bananas. Two bare-chested men moved it along
by punching poles to the river bottom.

Mrs. Sails signaled, calling,
"Here . . . here!" But they didn't hear.

"Oh bother!" grouched Mr. Sails.
"Going wrong way anyway."

Wheels crackled in the brush and sand.
Mrs. Sails jumped.

"The Vegetable Man! Of course—
it's Wednesday. He's to deliver a melon.
I hope he doesn't dally."

Mr. Sails moaned.

"Good morning, friend!" Mrs. Sails
called down.

The Vegetable Man bumbled up the ladder
and set down the melon.

"You're on your way to the city?" she asked.

"It's Wednesday!" he said.

She went on. "Mr. Sails"—
her rosy face flushed—"needs Red Rub.
One can buy it only at the city pharmacy.
You know, no?"

He nodded. "So . . . ?"

"It's near the city park." Her hands clasped
together as if praying. "These children can
purchase it . . . if they can tag along . . .
time's important . . . it's so far and weedy."
She added quickly, "Don't forget, you
promised a yellow squash from your garden."

"Oh."

He whipped around with a grumbly look.
"My horse is restless. Step lively . . .
that is, if you're going."

Pedro and Spud clattered down the ladder steps
behind him. It was hot, and the ride was bumpy.
Pedro was glad when Mr. Vegetable Man pointed.

"City pharmacy, one city block.
Midday—twelve o'clock—I'll return.
Be ready."

"Yes, sir," promised Pedro.

"Noonday," said Spud.

The wagon wobbled away, and they stood in
the city dazzle. Horns honked, cars scooted.

Painted white trees blurred.
Pedro's gaze chased up a pointy church steeple.

Just beyond, a pool and fountain flowed,
sparkling gold. A pink mist of water sprayed.
Bubbles gushed, streaming blue, purple.
The fountain looked like a lovely sea.
It was a sea, not deep, nor shallow.
The depth, Pedro judged, was only knee-deep.
Hot wagon scents still prickled his skin.

"Pedro?"

"Spud?"

They jumped in.
Delicious ripples of water swallowed them.
They rocked like sailboats, splashed like tugs.
In a splash, Pedro caught a bus driver's scowl.
An old woman shook her cane—
he scarcely noticed.

Instead, he cruised a river, then streamed on
out to sea.
From deep-sea bottom, he rose in pink bubbles.

Chapter 8

Ancient Coins

Pedro stood, shook himself, and looking up,
saw the Big Clock. Its chimes sounded now . . .
one . . . two . . . Pedro counted.

On *nine,* he remembered Mr. Sails.
On *ten,* he thought of Red Rub.
On *eleven,* he frowned.
On *twelve,* he gave a leap out of the water.

Then, before him, stepping high,
went three sailors singing smartly.

Their snappy steps sounded out a rhythm.
Their nautical hats sat just so,
and a snappish wind puffed shirts and britches.

The middle sailor's hat went flying,
soared, and breezed like a kite.

The middle sailor's hat went flying, soared, and breezed like a kite.

Then, lowering, it bumped over a car.
The three sailors howled.

"Crazy hat!" muttered Spud.

Pedro laughed. "Hat wants a chase."

People began to clap as the hat whammed
and slammed about.
Each time the middle sailor hurried to claim
his hat, the wind whooshed it away.

"I'll get it!" Pedro skittered up a tree trunk
and across a low limb.
There rested the hat, its power quite blown out.
"Game's up, hat," he told it.

He handed over the hat.

"Good job, mate!"

The middle sailor patted Pedro's head.
From his blue britches pocket,
he drew out two coins—
round, dark, knicked, and dull.

"Ancient money, mates!" he said.

Ancient money! In the big sea-worn hand,
the curious coins lay like treasure.

"Priceless," the sailor said.
"Got them from a sunken ship."

Bending over, whispering hoarsely, he said,
"Might be pirate money. Or possibly honest
money, earned by some poor sailor
swabbing the deck." He bent lower.
"That's for you to figure out."

He placed one coin in Pedro's hand,
the other in Spud's hand. Horns honked.
Folk crossed the street. A bicycle skimmed past.
The merry sailors stepped down the sidewalk,
singing again.

Spud yipped. "I didn't expect this."

Pedro gazed at his coin. Valuable?
Well, he'd hope! This piece had—without doubt—
sailed the seven seas. It was a fascinating piece,
dulled by time and briny water.

A horse snorted. Mr. Vegetable Man waited
at the curb. He sweated, red-faced. His wagon
creaked. The horse looked impatient to go.

"You're late," he said. "You have the
poor man's medicine? Get in . . ."

Pedro gulped. He'd forgotten about Red Rub.
The Big Clock chimed again.

"One o'clock! Didn't I say midday?"

Pedro's hand shot up to show
the ancient coin. "See?"

"Go get your Red Rub.
I'll hold your useless money."

They were soon back with red medicine in a sack.
Mr. Vegetable Man sat, nearly doubled,
gazing into his palm.

He handed back the coins.
"Useless, I say . . ."

Their wagon creaked onto the brushy river road.
At a stream, the thirsty horse drank.
Mr. Vegetable Man dipped his water crock.
Spud got a drink too.

Pedro kept gazing at his lovely coin. Bright
sunlight showed it as uncommon, etched deep.
Real treasure . . . or a poor man's pay?

He could hardly wait to show the Grandpoppa.
That man knew pirates, and he was acquainted
with the wealth of ships.

Soon they brushed against a banana tree
and waggled to a stop.

"Here's that bag of squash . . . hurry up,
if you want a ride home."
Spud stayed.

Delivery seemed fine work to Pedro.
Climbing up, he felt the sack's crinkles, and the
squashes' bumps. And deep inside his pocket—
the wonderful coin waited.
He tumbled onto the deck.
Nothing much had changed.
He handed over the two sacks.

"It's high time!" Mrs. Sails scolded.
"What took you two so long . . . ?"
She drew out the Red Rub.

Pedro's doings went round in his head, rushing
pell-mell. He'd gone sailing seas, chasing hats,
listening to sailors. He judged it best not to
mention that now. Instead, his fingers kept working
around the coin still in his pocket.

In haste, Mrs. Sails rubbed Red Rub onto
Mr. Sails's burning shoulder.

"Ooooh," he moaned, and
"mmmmm-hmmmmm," he murmured.

To Pedro, he said, "A Captain wears
the captain's hat only when he's kept
his word—to himself and to others."

Mrs. Sails smiled at Pedro, but she looked
rather sad. And the coin stayed deep, deep
down in the depth of Pedro's pocket.
He felt wilted, and a little sad too.

Chapter 9

Sailors at Tea

The purple bread wagon made a turn onto
a muddy road. Next to Mr. Bread Man
sat Mrs. Sails. Pedro and Spud were
squashed in like two lumps.

"Grandchildren are invited," Mrs. Sails
was saying. "These—especially for
today—are my grandchildren."

They came upon a rich river house.

"Ooooh!" gasped Mrs. Sails.

"Mmmm. Hmmmm,"
murmured Mr. Bread Man.

Around the elegant house wrapped a wide porch.
A red roof sparkled.
The plants stood about like guards.

The wagon wheels edged past
the old timbers of a boat.
It was splintered and split.
The half-rotted vessel lay sunken
and dirty in river mud.

"Pirates attacked," supposed Spud.

"No. Once it sank to bottom,"
said Pedro. But his heart said that
this was a craft for sailing.

The bread wagon stopped, and everybody got out.

"Your cake, Mr. Bread Man . . . it's
syrupy, sugared just right," said Mrs. Sails.
Holding the frothy cake high, she stepped
toward the porch.

"Dee-licious!" he promised,
and the bread wagon whisked away.

Then Pedro saw two boys.
The pair looked much like him and Spud.
Dark hair tumbled in dark curls.
Each had merry brown eyes.
Two red mouths curved just so.

"I'm Luc."

"I'm Marc."

"Hey, are you twins?" Spud burst out.

"Yes, are you?"

The question sent Spud into a joy spin.
Pedro laughed too.

In a glance at the porch, he saw a round table,
and on it a steaming teapot and cups.
Ladies in fancy dresses gathered.

A momma voice called,
"Boys, you can play in the old boat."

"Be careful. Watch for splinters."

"Don't fall into the river."

Pedro turned his full attention to
the old boat.
He saw boards, chunks, tar, roughness,
and washed pieces. Storms, winds, and
mean fish—this ship, no doubt, knew all.
He had to wonder about the Captain.

The boat's bottom sloped in mud.
Boards and cracks swelled.
Its lumber smelled muzzy like
a forest at noonday. And—
the whole was a dandy ship!

The four eager sailors stomped in.
That ship began an unpredictable journey.

Luc shinnied under a board.
"Can't find me!" he shouted.

Marc stood tall and searched the vast
water. "I'm searching for land."

Spud's arms swirled. "I'm
skee-doodling up the rigging."

Any sailor duty satisfied Pedro. There hung a
shred of lumber. He got under it.
He cat-walked along a ledge.
Staggering, came the Captain—
looking much like Spud.
Sea breezes whipped the yellow hair.

"Good sailing!" shouted Pedro.

The Captain needed a hat,
so Pedro drew one from the air
and fixed it on the yellow hair.
The two giggled and lurched
like seamen.

The brushy river road crackled.

"Pirates," whispered Luc hopefully.
"Get ready to fight."

Instead, an engine sputtered. In wobbled a wagon.

"Sail into any storms, mates?"
Mr. Bread Man joined their laughing.

For nourishment he gave each a round brown
muffin. At Tea's end, Mrs. Sails stepped back,
carrying a cake slice.

"Dee-licious! I brought a sample
for my hubby."

The four boys—sailors all—made a pact
to sail again.

"I'll climb rigging," said Spud.

"I'll man the big guns."

"Getting dark and cloudy,"
said Mrs. Sails. "Let's go home."

On the way Mr. Bread Man noted,
"Threatening clouds. Mean, purplish.
Expect a pounding, Mrs. Sails."

"Yes . . ."

Chapter 10

A Wash?

The ship house looked dark and lonely.
There, Mr. Sails leaned, watching their climb.

"Hurry!" he urged.
"Dirty weather's brewing."

Mrs. Sails handed up his slice of cake.

"Mr. Sails, cabin windows closed?"

"Closed!" He eyed the frothy cake.

"Every joint and seam nailed tight?"
she persisted.

He nodded, then tasted the icing.
"Inside!" he commanded.
He spoke like a Captain.

Lightning danced. Wind hissed at the ship's
circles, stacks, and squares. The gusts whipped
over ledges and loops. Sky came close,
boiling to huge, blue-black bubbles.

As Pedro figured, he stood smack in the middle
of a river storm! He wondered if this ship,
in a flash, might go afloat.

If so, Mr. Sails's goggly glasses would study
charts. Spud would twirl the wheel.
From the galley Mrs. Sails—certainly—
would serve up biscuits.
Likely, Pedro would search for lost ships.

"Just the usual thunderstorm," said
Mr. Sails. He finished off his cake.

Mrs. Sails stood and smoothed her
dress. "Sky's lighter. Rain's a mere
pitter-patter."

Mr. Sails announced, "Storm's over."

His wife eyed the closet door. "We've
a wash to do."

"Hmmm . . . perhaps," he murmured.

Out from the closet bumped a long laundry bag.
Mrs. Sails drizzled red soap into a cup.

"A wash?" protested Spud,
"but it's still raining."

"Drippy-drippy, and the sun's shining,"
she replied.

Mr. Sails licked his sticky fingers.
"Come, mates; watch Mrs. Sails's way
of doing the family wash."

He gave the bag a yank.
Mrs. Sails flung open the door.

"Oh!" gasped Spud.

"Yes!" cried Pedro.

Colors crisscrossed the rainy mist.
Raindrops pattered. Water covered just about
everything. The deck looked to be an ocean.

"It's the river, it's the sea!" Pedro cried.

The new rain layered the deck, enough for a small
swim. Pedro dipped deep till wetness swallowed
him. Raindrops bumped onto his shoulder.

Mr. Sails dumped the contents of the bag into the
deck sea. He rolled up his pant legs. Then,
snatching up the broom handle, he punched.
Towels and sheets sailed in a circle.

From the door, Mrs. Sails cheered.
Suds slathered the swimmers. Pedro bumped into
a red towel. Spud wrapped into a runaway sheet.
Their happy squeals sounded over river and forest.

When Pedro stood, he saw drippy circles,
sodden squares, drenched ledges,
and a lifeboat so squeaky clean, it sparkled.

"Laundry's clean," proclaimed Mr. Sails.
Wringing out each piece, he handed
it over to Mrs. Sails.

"My, you're doing a splendid job."

"Yes," agreed Mr. Sails as he snatched up
a purple towel.

A long sheet came billowing past. He got it.
As he wrung and handed each piece, she beamed.

"Mr. Sails, you're doing a Captain's job."

Pedro and Spud swam and splashed,
squealed and shouted. Well-rinsed sheets and
towels whirled past like boats.

It was true—Mr. Sails was doing a Captain's job.
Pedro ducked and came up spluttering.

But why wasn't that man wearing his Captain's hat?

Chapter 11

River Mud

Mr. Sails set down fishing line, spinner,
and a can of bait.

"Now as I'm told, we'll
go aboard that unusual boat there."
He pointed to the ugly-as-tar vessel.

"That old junker?" gasped Spud.
"Will it float?"

"Likely."

"It's old as pirates," said Spud.
"Positively crumbling."

Pedro gazed upon it.
"Where's the wheel?" he asked.

"I want to hear that engine," said Spud.

"You think it's got lifeboats?" asked Pedro.

Mr. Sails held out the three boarding tickets.
"Yes, that's it—*River Mud.*"

"*River Mud!*" Spud giggled.
"The name fits."

Pedro saw on it a crooked house
with a crooked walk and a humpbacked door.
So old, he'd expect whiskers.

Still, the vessel had a certain river-life air.
He liked it.

"*River Mud*'s sailing!" called a voice.

Mr. Fishing Boat's orange hair poked from under
his hat. His arms were muscled from twirling.

Pedro snatched up the bucket. Mr. Sails picked up
line, spinner, bait—and lunch. Spud eyed the
melon, then heaved it to his chest.

"Mind your step, friends,"
called Mr. Fishing Boat.

The plank wobbled and wavered, the bucket
swung, and the melon slid.

They stepped onto the dismal boat
that looked like a chicken coop.

Pedro saw rope, fire extinguisher,
a large jug of drinking water, wimpy life jackets,
and a knobby flashlight.

Fishermen in silly hats and wrinkly clothes
stomped in. Laughter rippled over the boat.

First off, Pedro found the driving wheel.
It appeared a solid old piece, notched, weathered—
and seaworthy. He wished to be the wheel twirler.
In that case, he'd swish this vessel past this river,
and right on out to sea.

    "We're sailing!"
    shouted Mr. Fishing Boat again.

The uncommon boat horn sounded.
More shuffles of feet came, more clanks of
buckets. The engine gained power.
River Mud rocked happily. Little boats scooted,
canoes glided past.

    "Water's shallow here," said Mr. Fishing Boat.
    "We're cruising into golden waters."

Their engine sputtered, then hushed.

"We're smack in the middle,"
Spud yelped.

"Fishing's splendid here,"
insisted Mr. Fishing Boat.

Mr. Sails's fishing line swung.
A rhythm of bobbing fishermen hats began.
All the seafaring people on the boat
settled into silence. Shapes and colors of fish
began spinning in.

"Yellow as a melon."

"Brown as a mud turtle."

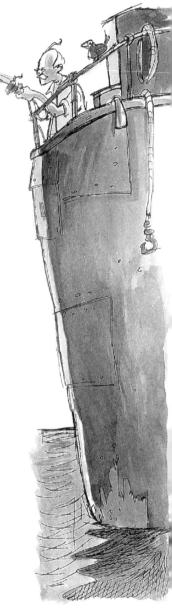

Spotted, dotted, silver fish flapped
into a large tub. Mr. Sails, however,
flung his catch into Pedro's red bucket.

Pedro caught more whiffs—
river wash, soppy shirts, bare toes,
and strong fish.
He drew in an aromatic sniff, and giggled.

They moved into warm wind.
The higgledy-piggledy boat
plowed through waves to where

the river narrowed.
A new excitement fell over their ship.

"We're entering a swamp of green wealth,"
promised Mr. Fishing Boat.

"Good," murmured Spud.

Pedro saw loops, logs, vines, and odd-shaped
trees. Greenery twined together, making a jungle.
Flowers poked out everywhere.
The river steamed soothingly.

"Remarkable," murmured Spud.
"See that steam, Pedro?"

"I think," Pedro whispered back—
"It's where the river comes to sleep."

"I often like snags and snarls," said Spud.

The muddy river darkened; tree roots widened,
thickening, looking more knotty.

Mr. Sails's final fish dangled into the bucket.
His goggly eyeglasses hung
on his second shirt button.
Glancing up, he took a sharp look ahead.

"Something's out there!" he hollered.

Chapter 12

Rescue

Mr. Fishing Boat tipped up his hat.
He gave the wheel a hard-handed whirl.
Everyone's talking hushed. On the dark river,
behind logs and loops, a shape blurred.

> "A stalled boat," pronounced the fisherman
> wearing green pants.

> The fisherman with sunglasses said,
> "It's a motor boat."

To Pedro, that smudge appeared a slice of orange,
a slash of white. He could make out two people.
One stood in the boat, waving.
The other hunkered.

> Leaning forward, Mr. Fishing Boat asked,
> "Is that a white flag?"

"No flag." The fisherman put on his
sunglasses again. "Not unless it's got arms.
 That flag's a white shirt."

"White shirt . . . mmmmm . . . somebody
needing help."

"A girl's waving it!" announced Spud.

Everybody rushed to see.
River Mud poked in close.
The white shirt fluttered, and the girl
motioned them in. They saw a man hunched
and holding his arm.

"Accident. Need first aid."
Her voice rang out over the swirly river.
"My brother cut his hand.
You have clear medicine? Bandages, no?"

"Medical supplies, yes!"
Mr. Fishing Boat shouted.

He snatched up a white box with a red cross.
He skimmed over the rail like a Captain.

"What's in that white box?"
Spud whispered.

"Medicine, bandages, little scissors,
and a knee-thumper," said Pedro.

Buckets and fishermen quieted while Mr.
Fishing Boat poured medicine.
The poor man yowled. The girl cringed.
Breezes blew her hair.
The *River Mud* bunch cheered.

"Thank you . . . oh . . . thank you . . ."

River Mud's engine snapped on.
The white box flew back to shelf.
The orange and white motor boat stirred the water.

"Be careful!"

"Work your way around logs."

"Beware of edges."

Good wishes sailed up and down.
Till the river bent, Pedro and Spud waved.

> Mr. Sails beamed. "Fine work," he said.
>
> "*River Mud* whipped into a Rescue Boat,"
> noted the fisherman in red pants.
>
> "A good turn always warms the heart,"
> noted the fisherman of the yellow shirt.

The fishing boat was making its way home.
Overhead trees shaded the river.
While washing through swirly currents of
splinters, rags, tatters, Pedro decided he'd
misjudged. This boat was no higgledy-piggledy
vessel. It was a fine seafaring ship—
a sailor's dream.

Soon they were tying in at the shore.

> Mr. Sails smacked his lips. "We'll chaw
> down tonight," he predicted. "Mrs. Sails,
> please get out the skillet."
>
> "Ashore—all who are going ashore!"
> shouted Mr. Fishing Boat.

Satisfied laughter ran over the boat. Feet shuffled,
buckets clanked, lines whipped.

Mr. Sails gathered their stuff.
He and Spud toted the bucket of fish.

When Pedro stepped on the plank, it wobbled.
Underneath, he saw goldfish.
Tea-colored water sloshed.

Midway on the plank, he paused to look back.
Mr. Fishing Boat's orange hair made
a patch under his Captain's hat.
He smiled at Pedro.

"Sail again, mate!"

Pedro nodded. Certainly he'd sail again.
And the next trip out, he might—possibly—
be the wheel twirler.
If things went along, he might—
some fine day—be Captain of a Rescue Boat.

Chapter 13

Drums on Parade

Mr. Sails wrapped mosquito netting around
Pedro's hammock.
Usually Mr. Sails took naps there, but tonight
this was Pedro's bed, on the ship house deck.

Spud had a net stretched over him and a red-white
quilt from Mrs. Sails. The two overnight guests lay
gazing up at the starry sky.

"I see an elephant, a tiger, and a chicken."

"I see an A; I see a B; I even see a Z."

"After a sleep will we get breakfast?"

"Mmmm," murmured Pedro.
"Mr. Milkman's milk waits in the
galley. Leja sent fresh butter."

Thank the nice folk, Leja had reminded them.
And watch out for mosquitoes. Pedro snuggled in.

Mosquitoes pestered the river, vexed the jungle,
and annoyed fishermen. But the pointy little
beasts wouldn't get Pedro.

At the near door Mr. Sails had set up
a sailor's bunk, and Mrs. Sails wasn't far away.
Feeling easy and safe, Pedro slept.

Next thing, Mr. Sails was tweaking at their toes.

> "Up for breakfast, mates! We're going
> fruit picking and nut gathering."

Pedro squinted at the sky, blue as a sea. Gone was
last night's black tent sky and all its sparklers.

> From inside, a voice rang, "Up, mates—"

> "Mrs. Sails—" Mr. Sails laughed—
> "she's such a hiker. Meets up with
> a red parrot, chats for hours.
> Weather and world events—
> oh, they get into such discussion."

Picturing this, Pedro untangled himself.
When he hit the deck, it sounded like *Thwack!*

The Grandmomma looked unusual.
Her long-legged trousers bagged, and her floppy
shirt billowed. Those oversized shoes would
make boats.

> Smiling, she greeted them,
> "Good morning, mates."

Sun bars splashed the galley table.
Mrs. Sails put out warm bread and yellow butter.
A knife and a banana went to each plate.
Hot coffee and steamy milk poured into four cups.

> Mr. Sails kissed his wife.
> "You're dressed fashionably, my dear."

> "Yes," she said.

After breakfast, Spud and Mr. Sails hurried
to put away bedding. Pedro tied up his tennis shoes.
Mrs. Sails packed a lunch.
Mr. Sails came swinging a laundry bag.

> "Here's a big bag for our fruit."

> "I hope we'll fill it," said Mrs. Sails.
> "Red, yellow fruit, wild grapes,
> papayas, mangoes—we welcome all."

"Nuts, any kind," said Mr. Sails.
"Soft-shelled, hard-shelled, brown,
orange, black . . ."

He patted his back pocket.
"Here's my knife for cutting the way."

The four clattered down the ladder steps.
They sloshed through beach sand.
Almost at once they entered a forest.

Pedro's shoes poked into moss
and slid across twigs.
When a log showed, he climbed over.

While the forest grew tall,
Pedro shrank.
And he felt runty again.
Paths tangled into hoses and twists.

Mrs. Sails gasped.
"Oh me, oh my!"

Before them towered
a mountain of a forest tree.
Its big bumpy roots spread like streams.
The wide leaves flapped.

"It's a giant." Mr. Sails gazed up at the tree.
"Cooling shade and a spot to rest my
 wobbly legs and tired back."

He settled himself over its broad roots.
Mrs. Sails drew out a water jar and four red cups.
Everybody drank.

Spud eyed a bird's nest. Mr. Sails snored,
his orange hat squashed against the tree.
His hiking shoes rested on a bumpy root.

The forest giant seemed a ship.
Branches climbed like rigging.
Dark leaves made wide masts.
Below, soft leaves and moss made a slimy sea.

Pedro knew a secret—such a secret,
that he resolved to keep it.
The broad pulpy roots of that giant tree
were hollow—like a drum!

He guessed no one else knew—
and he wouldn't tell. Not yet.

A yellow bird flew close, inviting a chase.
Spud followed.

Mrs. Sails picked blossoms. Mr. Sails snoozed.
It was hot too.

Pedro looked into the bird's nest.
Where had Spud gone?

　　"Spud!" Pedro called.

Spud had been gone too long.
Please call back, Pedro's heart begged.
Hearing no answer, he bumped down the path.

It was a troublesome path of gnarled roots,
old bark and vines. Along came a knotty log,
and Pedro sat upon it. His feet burned.
Wetness soaked his shirt and skin.

> When a battalion of insects moved in,
> he said, "Oh, get out."

Mr. Sails—in such a fix—would do
something wise. He would do a Captain thing.

But Pedro sighed. He wanted—
at this hot drowsy moment—only to sleep.

The forest floor would make a soft bed.
Moss and leaves would make a fine pillow.
Woods quieted. Pedro hurried himself up,
taking a few steps here and there.
Above treetops, a bit of sky showed.

Then a huge tree stopped him. Rising round, high,
and in a grand way, it looked a giant.
Bumpy humpy roots pushed out like ocean waves.

He gave a start.
Those healthy roots intrigued him.
Hollow—they were that, as fine and sturdy
as the world's best drum.

Such a thought came, so wise, so ideal,
that it set him bouncing.
And the secret of the giant tree—he'd give it away!
He, Pedro, would become a drummer.

A drummer needed drumsticks.
He began a search.
Mr. Bottle Man would use a hard bottle,
or perhaps, a strong shoe.

But heat and moisture had frizzled everything.
Ferns crumpled. Moss, twigs, bugs,
wet leaves—these had no strength.
He looked past stringly vines, around logs,
beyond, up, down, here, there.

Finally he found a broken tree limb,
short and stocky. A boy could swing it.

With energy he pounded the drum roots.
The piece bumped and banged.
He gave it effort and all his muscle.

A few birds returned his calls.
Snaps and snorts sounded. Some gnats gathered.
Any uncommon sound—he'd listen for it.

The roots got another good smacking.
He listened again. A smash in the brush,
he heard that.

"Pedro!" called Spud from far away.

"Pedro!"
In the afternoon mist stood Mr. Sails.
His orange hat cocked back,
the gray hair kinked.
"Good drumming, mate!" he cried.

Then Spud sloshed in.
He told them, "I went to sleep."

Crackling through brush, then,
came Mrs. Sails.
She folded Spud into her perfumy shirt.
"I'm glad you're found."

Spud looked down, then he skittered over
to take a whack on the root.
The beating made echoes across the forest.

Mr. Sails clapped. "Sounds a parade!"

Mrs. Sails cried, "Celebration!"

Certainly, thought Pedro.

Mr. Sails whipped out lunch.
"Boiled eggs, cheese, our good
Bread Man's loaf."

The jar of purple jelly found its way
to the spread tablecloth.
They ate, then tossed crumbs to birds.

"All's well that ends well," said Mrs. Sails,
and she gathered their empty cups.

Toting their bags, the four headed slowly
for the ship house.

"Such a day," said Spud. "We met a giant."

"Enjoyed a parade," said Mr. Sails.

"Drum beating told Spud your place,"
pointed out Mrs. Sails.
"Sensible, clever," she said.

"Thought out a plan . . . performed it,"
added Mr. Sails. "Pedro, you should wear
a Captain's hat."

Flipping off his orange hat, the Grandpoppa
squashed it grandly onto Pedro's head.

"Hey!" Pedro gasped. He reached up to
touch it. The hat felt warm, damp, wrinkly,
and a hat to be worn in honor.

He tapped the rim and no longer felt runty.
Instead he felt cheery—someone of immense
wealth and worth.

The forest whispered and whirred.
It sighed and sang.
They walked past leaves of gold and amber,
sea-green trees, pea-green trees,
vines, and flowers bright as cherries.

The whole was a parade—Pedro's parade.

Chapter 14

Waterfront Dash

The waterfront looked like a big circus.
Pink cotton candy fluffed past, and popcorn
was sprinkled around. Three new balloons
sailed over people's heads.

Immediately Pedro picked out the Grandpoppa
and Grandmomma. They stood at water's edge.
Between them rested a twisty bundle.

"Mrs. Sails with her sails!"
yelped Pedro to Spud. "Let's go!"

"Halloo, halloo," greeted Mr. Sails.
Patting the bundle, he said, "Mrs. Sails
stitched the jags and tatters. These"—
he winked—"will put money
into her apron pocket."

Then, hurrying away, the two disappeared
through the stone building door.

The big waterfront thumped. Dockworkers
yelled, and men toted pipes.
Barrels went rolling. Cotton bales flopped.

Such hullabaloo—where could Pedro look?
He stood between shoreline and shops,
then he spun himself around.

Stopping, opening his eyes, he saw a friend—
someone he greatly admired.
Wearing her flower basket like a hat,
the Flower Lady stepped along the pier.
Tiny vines and blooms trailed down her dark hair.
Blue bells, yellow wheels, purple pinks
made a hanging bouquet.
White petals sprinkled the bunch.

She smiled at him, then gasped, "Ooooh!"
Her basket nearly slipped.
"Oh no!" she cried out.

Pedro and Spud ran to see.

"Good friends . . ." Grasping her skirt,
she moaned. "Look—an old pier nail
ripped this skirt hem."

She gazed down at the rip, as if it were
a great grief.
"I brought no needle, no thread," she wailed.
"Whatever will I do?"

Pedro and Spud studied the jagged seam.

"I don't know as you can fix it,"
Spud said.

Pedro thought, If only there were a needle,
a bit of thread . . .

"But I'll look so mussed. Who will buy
my lovely flowers?"

Pedro thought she might cry.
He stared across the pier, around barrels, over bales,
rolling equipment, pipes, and anchors.

Shoppers, sellers, dockworkers, fishermen,
and sailors made a multitude. But who—
in this crowd—might have a needle on hand?
Who might have thread?

Pedro set off in a run, Spud close behind.
First off, he saw—between peanut wagon and
lemonade cart—a rich man.

At least he judged him to be rich,
with his hair that wavy and his shoes that brilliant.
Pedro scooted in, but he felt runty.

"Excuse, sir. Please a needle?
And some thread?"

The rich man chuckled.
"Needle and thread? Sorry, friend.
My suits are well stitched."

Pedro hurried to the smoking peanut wagon.

"Please, sir . . . would you have a
needle . . . some fine thread?"

The peanut man laughed. "Who, me?
Hot peanuts and a burny cart—those are
my earthly possessions."

A red balloon sailed, catching Pedro's eye.
He hurried over. But the man had yet
three green ones to blow. It seemed useless to ask.

A fisherman muttered, "Sorry, mate.
Hooks, lines, bait—that's my day's work."

A lady walking her dog said, no, she had only
her pet and a pink leash.

A lady walking her dog . . .

Stumping over boards, Pedro smelled tar,
boat glue, and lumber. The whole smelled of iron,
river wash, and rust. He leaned on a barrel, panting.

To his left, he saw Mrs. Sails seated in a wicker
rocker, fanning. Mrs. Sails delighted in stitching.
But she used coarse thread and a brawny needle.
Still . . . He made a dash.

"A needle . . . thread . . ." he begged.
"The Flower Lady's skirt hem . . ."

"Oh my!" cried Mrs. Sails.
"A nail, I imagine."

She reached into the lacy pocket of her dress.

"Needles—I carry every size . . .
Thread—coarse, fine . . . very fine."

Holding the tiny tools, Pedro ran.

"Get out of the way, barrels and bales!"
he yelped.

He and Spud slid to a stop in front of
the Flower Lady.

"Ah, yes," she murmured. "A friend in need
is a friend indeed."

She pushed thread into the tiny needle
and her capable fingers worked over the torn hem.

"Thank you, you lovely children."

Again, along the pier, stepped the Flower Lady.
Pinks, blossoms, wheels, and bells curved into a
rainbow. The colors streamed down her shiny hair.

"Back to Mrs. Sails's dress pocket,"
Pedro told the needle and wisp of thread.

From here, he viewed Mrs. Sails,
still rocking and fanning—
and rosy in her lilac dress.
Nearby stood Mr. Sails.
But—who was that personage,
that distinctive important gentleman
speaking with him?

Pedro took another look.
Sunshine sparkled on the man,
on his handsome uniform, and mostly—
on the gold and white hat.

Chapter 15

The Captain's Hat

"Spud!" Pedro gasped.
"There's a Captain!"

"Let's go!"

The Captain grinned.
"These mates yours?"

"Oh, yes," said Mrs. Sails. "Why, we've practically adopted these children. Before they found our ship house, our lives were so quiet and peaceful. A bit ho-hum perhaps, but now . . ." She laughed.

The Captain gave a merry laugh too,
and he shook hands.
He told Pedro and Spud about his ship,
his sailors, the deck, the engines,
and the ship wheel.

"Oh," said Spud.

"Oh," said Pedro,
and he put away the words in his heart.
Tonight while he and Leja drank milk,
he would tell all that he'd heard.

When the Captain strolled away, Mrs. Sails stood.

"Kindly Mr. Vegetable Man's giving us all
a ride home. Four o'clock." She hurried
into the broom and sausage shop.

Mr. Sails ordered popcorn.
The three sat down under the sign *Cafe.*
Spud and Mr. Sails went to watch boats.
Pedro munched popcorn and observed
the Captain's doings.

The Captain waved to his sailors.
It amazed Pedro, the way a Captain
could get around. That man seemed to be
anywhere—everywhere—on the waterfront.

He helped a tottery old gentleman
to a chair. He stepped aside, so folk could pass.

A blind musician played the violin.
The Captain paused to listen, and after,
put money into the cup.

Seeing the Flower Lady, the Captain
tipped his hat. He chose a pretty bouquet.
He took a few steps across the pier
and handed the posies to an old lady.

Bales and boxes thumped the pier.
Dockworkers scrambled around. Two shirtless
men toted a long iron pipe. The Captain kept
stepping aside and didn't seem to mind.

As Pedro figured, a Captain nodded, assisted,
or got out of the way. And he waved to his sailors.

The bright, noisy waterfront held Pedro in a daze.
Then—oh, that surprised him—the Captain
sat in a chair at the next table.
Off came the elegant Captain's hat.
The marvelous golden hat went to the table.

Pedro had a chance to observe—and to wonder.
That hat intrigued him.

At night, where went the Captain's hat?
When a storm raged, where went that hat?

Pedro's imagining ran on and on.
In a tossing ship . . . what then?
If cold winds blew, if a storm fussed . . .
whatever did the hat do?

The Captain saw his daydreaming.

> "Hey, mate! You're spunky," he said.
> "I saw you helping a lady in distress,
> the Flower Lady." His smile widened.
> "You chased all over this waterfront."

His smile seemed a gift. The words made little
bounces over the hat on the table. The bounces
settled over Pedro.

> The Captain eyed Pedro's head.
> "Fine hat, mate!"

Pedro touched the orange hat,
still squashed on his head.
Mr. Sails's hat—
received for root-thumping rescues.

> The Captain got up, tapped on his hat,
> and strolled off. "Good sailing, mate!"

Pedro wadded up his popcorn sack.
Mr. Sails and Spud sauntered in.

Out came Mrs. Sails, carrying
a brown sausage.

   "Four o'clock," she told them.

Mr. Vegetable Man's wagon creaked in . . .
on the minute. Mr. Sails assisted his wife
up to the wagon seat. Spud squiggled in
among the cucumbers.
Pedro brought Mr. Vegetable Man a cool drink.
With everybody aboard, the wagon started.

   "Good sailing!" shouted Pedro
   in his most merry Pedro voice.

He meant the ship and the vegetable wagon.
He spoke for the Captain and all the sailors.

The wagon wobbled. It screaked.
The sleepy horse poked along.
Pedro dreamed his hat was shiny gold.
And everybody hummed to the rhythm
of the road, the river, and the sea.